This Tree Is Just For ME!

Lucy Rowland

Laura Hughes

BLOOMSBURY
CHILDREN'S BOOKS

LONDON OXFORD NEW YORK NEW DELHI SYDNEY

Jack was excited! He had a new book.

He hunted around for a small, quiet nook . . .

But out in the garden, the blackbirds were tweeting,

the woodpecker pecked and the squirrels were eating!

"Oh how can I read with this racket?" Jack groaned.

He told them, "I'm finding a tree of my own."

"Not THIS tree," said Jack, "it's a little bit small.

And this one
is wobbly.

This one's too tall!"

But there, in the corner, as calm as could be –
the most perfect place!

"Oh, THIS tree's just for ME!"

Jack sat in his tree
without making a sound,
swinging his feet,
peering down at the ground...

And ever so happily
reading his book . . .

till all of a sudden
the tree branches SHOOK!

And, way up above him, Jack saw something jump.
A tiger arrived on his branch with a THUMP!
A *tiger?* Good grief! And he wanted to chat!
But this was *Jack's* tree. No, he couldn't have that!

Jack **ROARED!** with the tiger

(it felt rather good!)

then told him, "I'm sorry, I'd play if I could,
but I'm reading my book
and the thing is, you see,
I'm not being rude,
but **this tree's just for ME.**"

So Jack felt **quite pleased** till a few moments later
he turned to discover... a large **alligator!**

Jack did some SNAPPING – (yes, that was **quite fun!**) –
until he **remembered** the book he'd begun.

"This tree's just for ME and I'm reading my book!"

Then, high up above, a *new* sound made Jack look...

And "Hiss!" hissed the snake as she slithered along.
"I'm reading," sighed Jack. Oh dear! This was all wrong!
But he WRIGGLED and SLID (and he had to agree,
it was quite a fun game)...

"But **this tree's
just for ME!**"

Jack waved the snake off
and he'd **just** settled down,
when the leaves began **moving**!
Jack started to frown...

A *monkey*?! They HUNG
and they SWUNG in the tree...

till, firmly, Jack told him,

"This tree's just for ME!"

At last! Peace and quiet! By hook or by crook,
Jack was determined to finish his book.
But what was that SNORING? A sloth napped nearby.
She stretched out her arms and she gave a big sigh.

A snooze was quite tempting, Jack had to agree!
But he poked the sloth gently: "This tree's just for ME!"

"I can't fall asleep," Jack explained,
"because – look!
I'm trying to finish . . ." (he yawned)
"my new book."

He'd just turned the page
when there started a din.
"What now?" grumbled Jack,
as he scratched at his chin.

A *bear*? And some *penguins*?

An *elephant* too?

Jack's nice **quiet** tree
sounded more like a
ZOO!

"I'm reading my book —
I *must* make them all see!"
So he **shouted**
(quite rudely)...

"THIS trees's

The bear looked quite shocked
and the penguins all frowned.

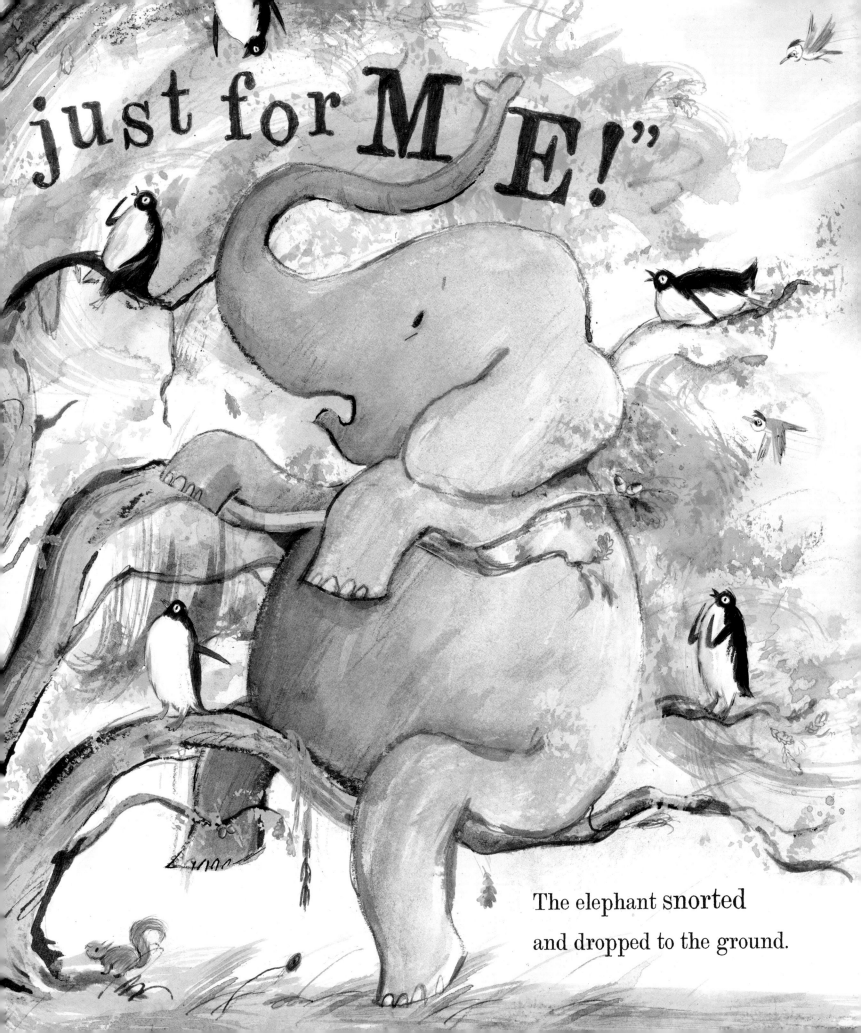

just for M E!"

The elephant snorted
and dropped to the ground.

"At last!" smiled Jack. It was calm as could be!
So he finished his book... in his **very own** tree.

But now it was quiet,
it wasn't the same.

Jack hoped for another new noise...

... but none came.

"A tree just for *me*?" Jack stood up really tall, then shouted,

"Come back! It's a tree for us ALL!"

Swinging . . .

and climbing,

Jack giggled, "Who knew?

A tree is **much** better
with **friends** in it too!"

And books are *more* fun
when you're reading aloud –
in a **tree for us ALL**
to a very big crowd.